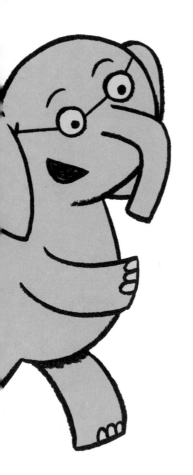

An ELEPHANT & PIGGIE LIKE READING! Book

Hyperion Books for Children / *New York*

AN IMPRINT OF DISNEY BOOK GROUP

For Sarah—who is always fun to do nothing with.

First Edition, May 2017 • 1 3 5 7 9 10 8 6 4 2 • FAC-029191-17034 • Printed in Malaysia

Reinforced binding

This book is set in Century 725, Futura/Monotype; Grilled Cheese/FontBros; Typography of Coop, Fink,
Neutraface/House Industries

Library of Congress Cataloging-in-Publication Data
Names: Willems, Mo, author, illustrator. | Harper, Charise Mericle, author,
  illustrator.
Title: The good for nothing button! / by [Mo Willems and] Charise Mericle Harper.
Description: Los Angeles ; New York : Hyperion Books for Children, an imprint
  of Disney Book Group, [2017] | Series: Elephant & Piggie like reading! |
Summary: "Yellow Bird has found a button and wants to share it with Red Bird and Blue Bird. This is just an
ordinary button. It does not do anything when you press it. But when Red Bird and Blue Bird give it a try, they
are delighted to find that the button does not do nothing, and that is something!"—Provided by publisher.
Identifiers: LCCN 2016013603 | ISBN 9781484726464 (hardback)
Subjects: | Buttons—Fiction. | Birds—Fiction. | Humorous stories. |
  BISAC: JUVENILE FICTION / Concepts / General. | JUVENILE FICTION /
  Humorous Stories. | JUVENILE FICTION / Social Issues / Values & Virtues.
Classification: PZ7.W65535 Gq 2017 | DDC [E]—dc23
LC record available at http://lccn.loc.gov/2016013603

Visit hyperionbooksforchildren.com and pigeonpresents.com

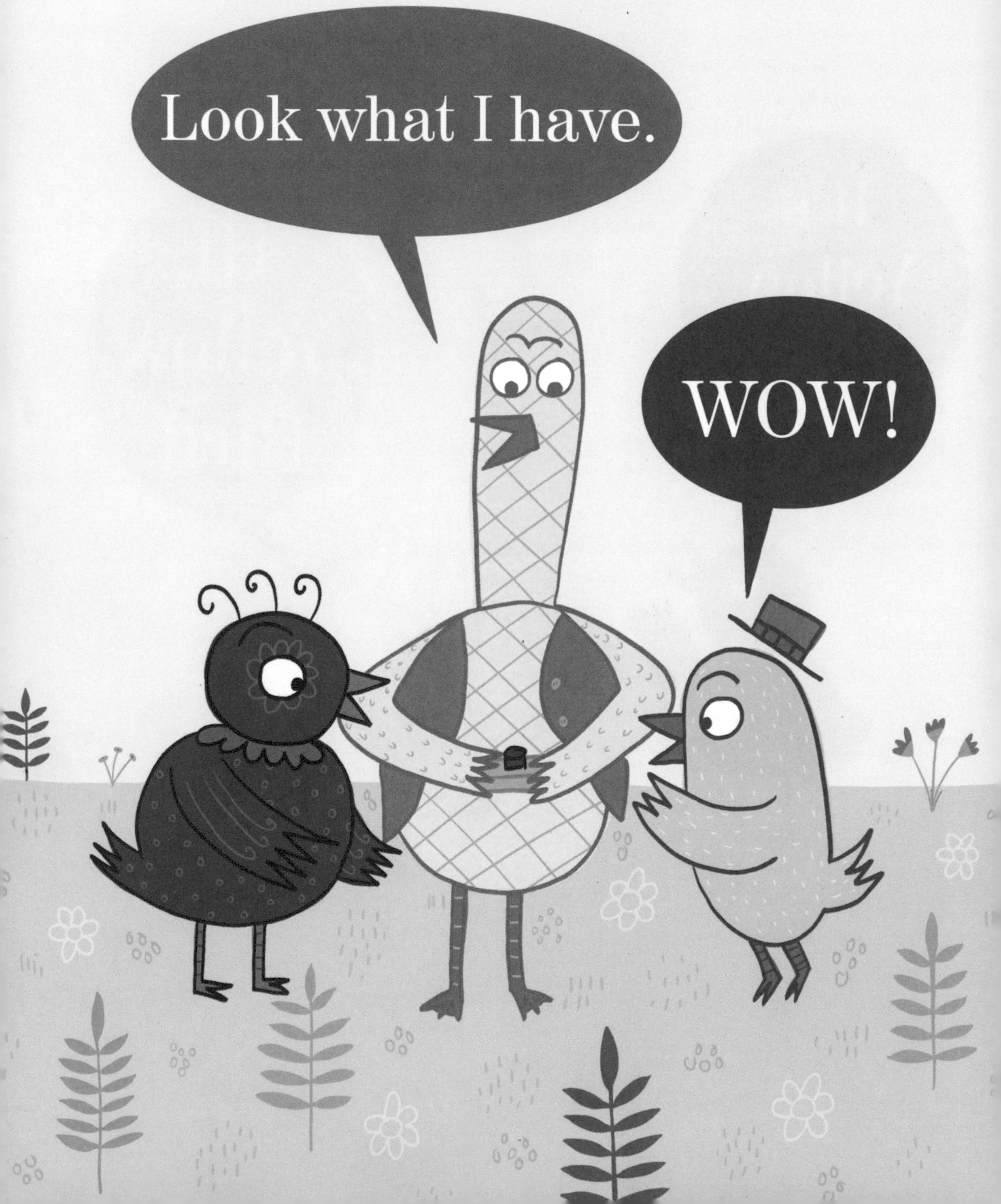
Look what I have.
WOW!

7

9

11

13

21

27

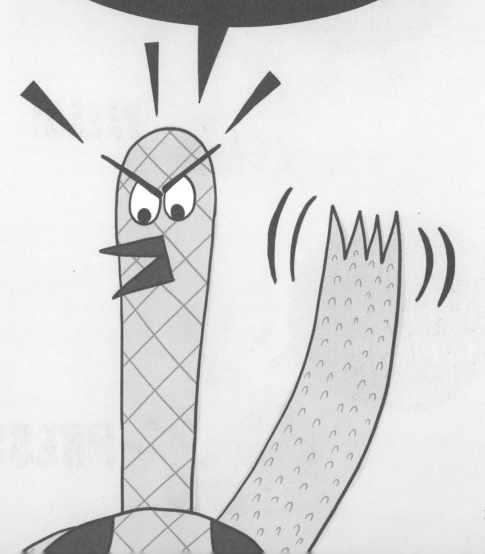

37

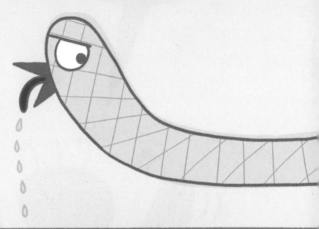

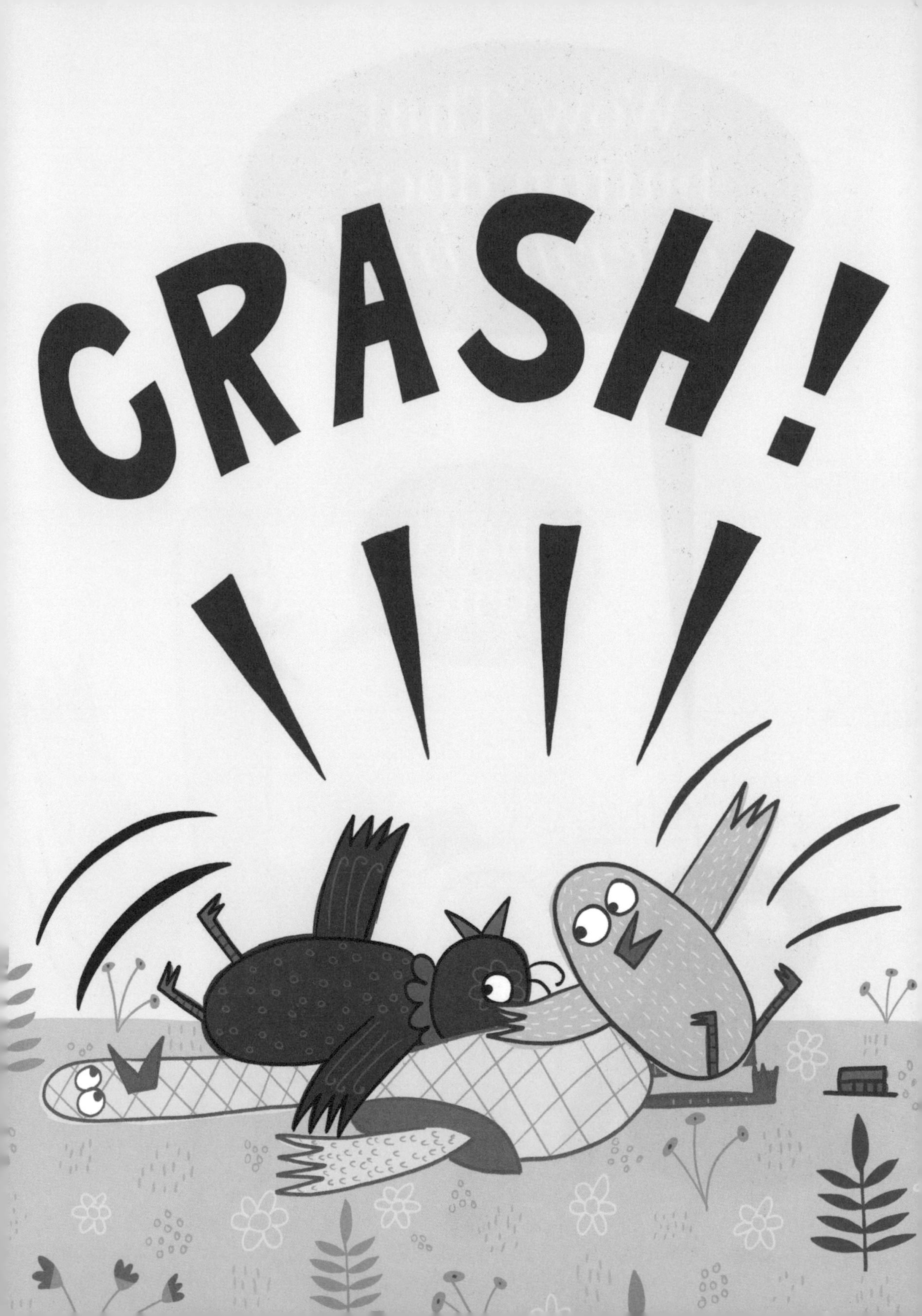
CRASH!

49

Elephant & Piggie also like reading:

The Cookie Fiasco
by Dan Santat

We Are Growing!
by Laurie Keller